Goodnight Bunny

WaterMark, Inc.

WaterMark, Inc.

Text © 2005 Hollins University
Illustrations © 2005 Sweetwater Press
Published in cooperation with Sweetwater Press
Produced by Cliff Road Books

Printed and bound in Italy
Book design by Miles G. Parsons

ISBN 1-88207-762-8

Goodnight Bunny

Margaret Wise Brown
Illustrated by Beth Foster Wiggins

Once upon a time, in a hollow stump
Lived one sleepy bunny with
One sleepy mother and
One sleepy father and

Two sleepy sisters and
Three sleepy brothers and

Four sleepy uncles and
Five sleepy aunts and

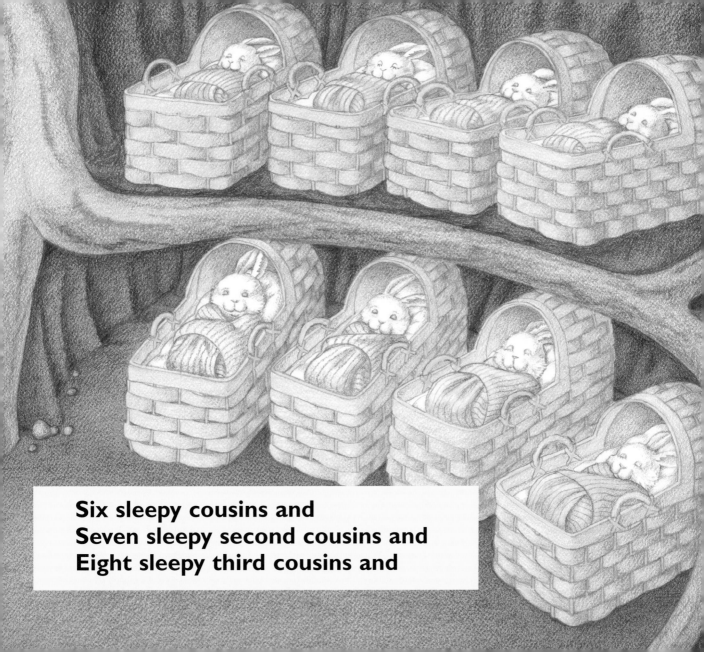

Six sleepy cousins and
Seven sleepy second cousins and
Eight sleepy third cousins and

Two sleepy grandmothers and
Two sleepy grandfathers and

Four great grandmothers and
Four great grandfathers and

**Eight great great grandmothers and
Eight great great grandfathers and**

Sixteen great great great grandmothers and
Sixteen great great great grandfathers and

One sleepy bunny doll made out of a carrot —
It didn't last long.

They were a big warm rabbit family, all in one clump
And they all lived together in a hollow stump

With a little sleepy bunny who was just learning
how to jump.